What the readers say:

"I found this book really funny and exc̲ ̲ ̲ ̲ ̲ ̲ ̲ ̲ ̲ ̲ ̲ ̲ ̲ good level of scariness."

- Hugo age 9

"I really enjoyed this book because it is very interesting and magical."

- Etienne age 9

"I really enjoyed this book since it was funny, witty and had exciting mysterious parts."

- Annica age 10

"I liked reading this book because it was full of action and mystery."

- Sermed age 10

"This book is the best book ever because it was interesting from beginning to end and had really funny characters."

- Leila age 10

"This book was really good because it has happy parts and scary parts."

- Nela age 10

"This is a really interesting and exciting book because the adventures give you the shivers. I recommend this book to people of all ages."

- Piotr age 10

'Darkness will cover up the light,
Ash will fill your world,
Look for hope,
Look for heroes.'

Book of Eran: Chapter 7, Verse 23

The Icewalker Chronicles

Book 1
Dragon Land

Chapter 1
- The Kingdom

A time long ago, in a land far away, lived a boy called Mondo. Mondo had two friends called Tommy and Jenny, who were twins. The three children liked to practise magic but none of them were very good. Jenny and Tommy were always trying to change objects around, a bucket into a chair, an ink pen into a stamp, that sort of thing. Mondo, on the other hand, had his mind set on a different type of magic; he tried to control the water particles in the air and bring them under his control.

The world the three children lived in was called Valerian. It was a magical, enchanted place with both good and evil magic. You could often see a fairy flying around, leaving a trail of magic dust behind it. Most of the people in Mondo's home town of Lavenville worked as farmers or blacksmiths, making swords or shields for the great King of the land, Zoltar. Their kingdom was very beautiful, with luscious forests and green fields stretching out as far as the eye could see. Most of the land was covered in forests, plants and lakes.

The only problem with their kingdom was
the evil magic; it tempted men with powers
beyond their control. It seemed that no matter
how great a kingdom is, evil will always try to
find a way to ruin things.

Chapter 2
- Mondo

"*W*ake up Mondo. It is time to practise your magic." Mondo awoke to the sound of his grandfather's wise but strange voice calling up the stairs but he was still very tired. Like all nine year old boys he knew, being nine was all about sleeping, not studying. Mondo preferred it when he was asleep as he could dream about fighting big dragons and monsters.

Mondo's grandfather was always the one to wake him up every morning. *It seems like he never sleeps,* Mondo thought to himself. Mondo's grandfather was the wisest person he knew; he had travelled the whole kingdom and had been on many adventures. Mondo's grandfather also knew a lot about magic and spells as he had been studying hard his whole life. He was the one who had always pushed Mondo to practise. He would say, "You'll thank me one day," Always that line, nothing more, nothing less.

He looked like your typical old man really: Long white hair, a white beard in a ponytail and long, loose robes. The only thing different about him was his eyes. His eyes would always tell you something.

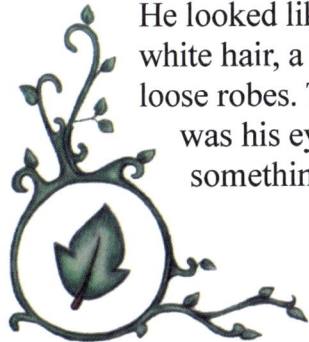

Sometimes when he was speaking his eyes would tell you something else, and sometimes when he was not speaking his eyes would tell you something.

Like every other morning, Mondo went out and started practising his magic. The best time of the day to practise was always the morning because the dew from the previous night was still on the tips of the grass. Mondo would always start by making the drops of dew dance around and then use them to form different shapes and objects.

Mondo was extra excited that day because a travelling fair was coming to town and even King Zoltar himself was going to watch! The fair was called 'Thornzan's Happy Circus'. The only strange thing about this circus was that Mondo had never heard any good things said about it at all. News normally travelled fast and far in Valerian because traders and wanderers commonly moved between the towns. However none of the travellers had said anything good about this circus. Come to think about it, nobody had said anything at all about this circus.

Chapter 3
– The Meeting

*T*hat afternoon, the circus rolled into town. Mondo was playing by a big oak tree with Tommy and Jenny when the carts rolled past. On the side of the wagons, written in big red letters, read *'World Famous, Thornzan's Happy Circus'*. The writing really stood out to Mondo as the background was all in black.

As the wagons rolled past, one of the drivers caught the eye of Mondo and his friends and stopped the cart. The big, strange man, dressed all in black and red, peered down at the children and gave a big grin.

"Hello," the man said in a deep, sly voice.

"Hello!" replied the children excitedly.

"My name's Thornzan but you can call me Thorn. Will you be coming to the circus this evening?" he asked.

"Oh yes!" replied Tommy and Jenny, but Mondo stood silently.

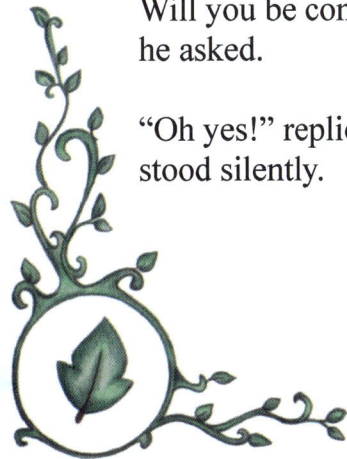

"Good. Good!" said Thorn. "We wouldn't want anyone to miss *this* show. We want everyone to be there!"

Thornzan laughed and with that, his carriage began to roll away. The cart that Thornzan was driving was covered by a big, black sheet and on the sheet was written 'Main Event' in red letters.

Excitement rose throughout the day as the town prepared itself for the circus. Signs went up everywhere 'Starts 4pm' 'Entrance 30zek'. Everyone in town was going; even the royal chair was being made ready for King Zoltar. Mondo had

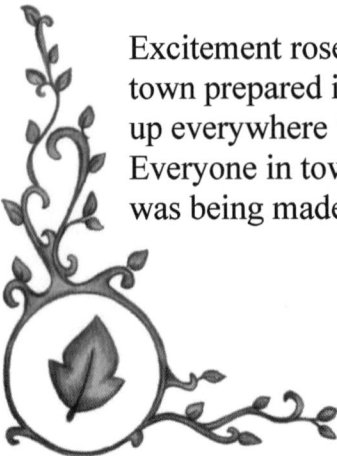

a funny feeling in his stomach though after meeting Thornzan. What did he mean 'It's good to have everyone together', and why did he laugh with that grin at the end? He went to talk to his grandfather about his feelings and ask for advice. After Mondo had explained to his grandfather all that had happened, the wise old man took a big inhale from his pipe and thought for a moment.

"Thornzan you say... Hmm. Have you been practising your magic?" Grandad asked in a curious tone.

"Yes!" Mondo replied.

"Well, that's all you need to worry about," Grandad replied and then he said no more.

To Mondo this meant absolutely nothing, but he would never question his grandfather. It obviously meant something very wise.

Chapter 4
- To The Circus!

*T*he afternoon was beginning to come to an end, and a cool breeze picked up in the air as the sun started to slip over the horizon. Mondo was finishing a game of chess with his grandfather and, as they were about to set off to the circus, Mondo's grandfather said, "You go meet Tommy and Jenny; I have a few things I need to do first. I'll meet you down there later."

Mondo was still feeling slightly worried as he set off for the circus. He ran down the sloping path that led him to the town centre. As he rounded the corner, and the town came into view, the sheer size of the event struck him like a blow to the head. The outside marquee was enormous, probably the biggest he had ever seen.

There were people from all over Valerian; there must have been thousands of people! Mondo walked through all the outside stalls, which were selling candy and drinks, and entered the circus. Inside the circus tent Mondo met Jenny and Tommy; they had agreed beforehand where to meet because they knew the event was going to be really big. Mondo couldn't see his grandfather anywhere, but the show was about to start.

"Hey, come on! The show is about to begin." Tommy shouted.

They took their seats and prepared themselves for the show. As Mondo looked around, he still couldn't see his grandfather. While looking around, he also noticed that the whole circus was just in two colours, black and red. However, his worries

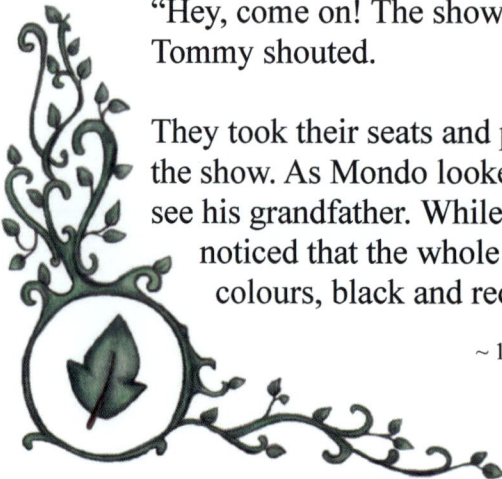

quickly washed away and Mondo found himself quite excited as the show began.

The lights inside the circus dimmed and a magic show began. There were all kinds of tricks happening during the performance. The children watched people performing with animals; some of these animals Mondo had never seen before. There were magicians transforming all kinds of solid objects into liquids or gases, and there were jesters blowing out fire, making the fire dance around. Tommy was on the edge of his seat and jumped up and down with excitement. Jenny, on the other hand, looked like she had seen it all before. It was clear to the three of them that these jesters had been practising their magic for a long time. How exciting the show was becoming!

As the circus drew to a close, the Ring Master entered the centre of the arena. It was Thornzan. He settled the crowd and announced to the audience that they were ready to perform the final trick. Thornzan asked if King Zoltar would come to the front to be involved in the final trick. The King's advisers were very wary and advised the King against participating. However, the proud warrior King, who had conquered many realms with his bare hands, stood up and started to walk proudly towards the stage. The entire crowd watched with excitement as the King walked onto the stage.

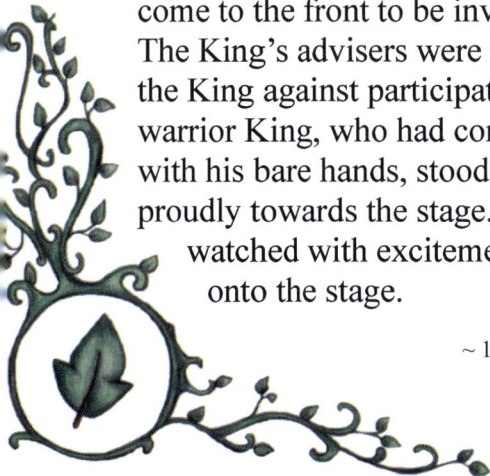

"This final trick is called *The Black box*" Thornzan said. He then looked at the King and whispered "Don't worry, it's only a name."

The King was placed inside a big wooden box which was standing in front of the still concealed main event wagon, which Mondo remembered from before. Thornzan then asked the crowd to count down from 10. The excited crowd starting counting down 10, 9, 8, 7, 6, 5, 4, 3, 2, 1, BOOM!!!

With that, the King disappeared and fireworks shot into the sky of the tent! The crowd went crazy with applause but Mondo jumped to his feet.

"He's gone!" he said, "He's gone!"

Suddenly, the roof of the tent opened and red fireworks shot into the early evening sky.

Mondo whispered to Tommy and Jenny, "We've gotta go!"

Suddenly, the cheers from the crowd changed into panic and cries came screaming out. The friendly jesters and Thornzan turned towards the crowd and started firing magic bolts at them. From the sealed main event box, a giant, ferocious, red dragon burst out and took to the evening sky. The King's advisors and knights were helpless against the power of all of Thorn's army. The full force of the

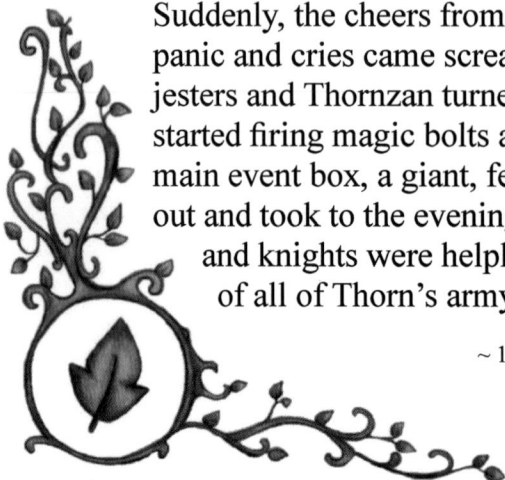

King's army were only ever called together when war was declared, so they stood no chance with so many against so few.

Mondo, Tommy and Jenny quickly tried to escape but, as they were thinking of a plan, the dragon swooped down for his first attack. Red hot fire came bursting out from the dragon's mouth as it flew straight towards all the people sitting around Mondo, Tommy and Jenny. Mondo, faster than he had ever done before, mastered up all his strength and created a dome of ice which shielded him and all the people sitting around them. As the fire struck against the dome of ice, Mondo looked at Tommy and Jenny and screamed, "DO SOMETHING!"

Like they had awoken from a dream, Jenny changed
the wooden floor below them into a trap drop
and the three of them sneaked under the wooden
seating, ran out of the circus tent and into the nearby
woods. Unfortunately for them, they did not escape
unnoticed.

Chapter 5
– The Woods

*I*n the dark woods, the screams from the tent were still ringing out. The children quickly realised that the possibility of anyone surviving out there was slim at best, for their land was not full of warriors and magicians but simple working folk. Another thing the children realized was that they were now very much alone.

"What shall we do now?" asked Tommy.

"We must hide till morning," replied Mondo.

As the group started to look around, to find somewhere to hide for the night, they heard the noise of a group entering the woods. Was it survivors? Was it the circus? Was it just an animal? They didn't know, so they decided to continue to prepare their hiding space anyway. Mondo had a great idea to make the water on the ground form into a path of footprints of the three children, walking away from where they were hiding. Tommy also changed the leaves around them into a blanket.

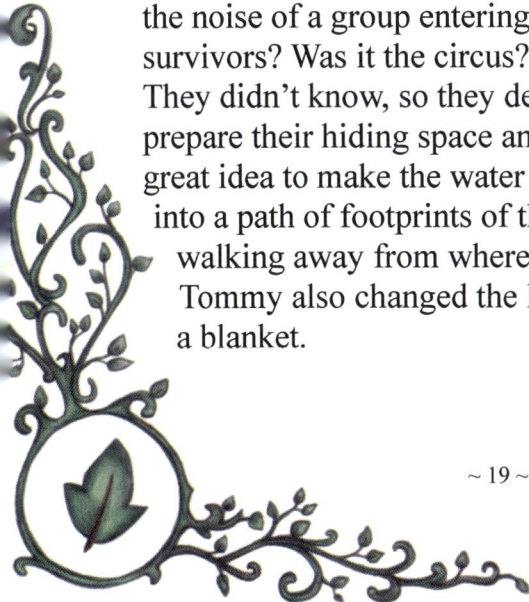

"Hey guys, look what I made! It's a blanket that we can lie under so we blend in with the rest of the forest," Tommy said proudly.

As the three started to lie down under the net, the sound of the group came closer.

Tommy whispered, "Quick hide!"

The mysterious group approached and their noises became louder and louder. It was clear now that this group were not survivors. As the group came to the area where the three children were hiding, the children could see through the small holes in the blanket of leaves that the noises had come from a group of jesters. The group looked very different now, very evil and determined.

"We must find those boys!" one of the jesters said.

"Boss will be mad with us if we don't," said another.

The group now stopped where the children were lying and looked around for them. One of the jesters started pressing his foot around on the ground, trying to feel for something strange. As his foot was just about to step on Jenny, one of the other jesters shouted.

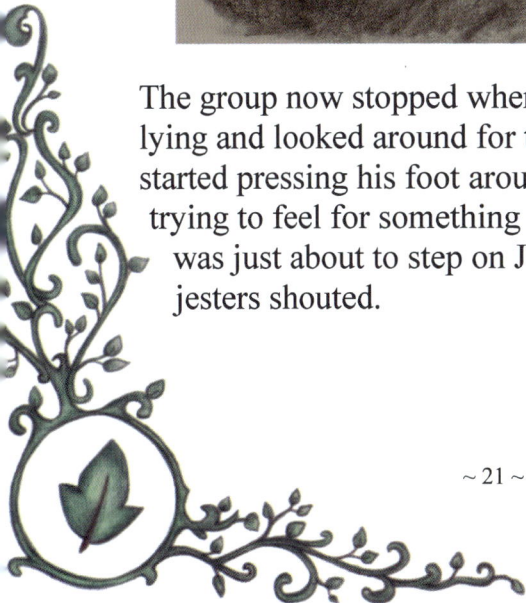

"Over here! I found their foot prints. We've got them now!" and the group of jesters went hurdling off into the distance.

The children gave out a big sigh of relief. The chaos seemed like it had stopped and the three children looked at each other and reflected on what had just happened. They were all surprised and pleased with what they were able to do with their magic under such intense pressure. Exhausted, the three of them soon fell asleep.

Chapter 6
– The Next Day

*T*he group awoke to an early, wet forest, the horrors of the night before still fresh in their minds.

"What do we do now?" asked Jenny.

Both boys said noth ing for a while. Finally Mondo said, "We have to go back to the town and see what it looks like."

The group agreed. They decided to leave the forest and set off back to where the circus had been the night before. As the group walked past the last trees on the edge of the forest and entered the vast open field again, they saw that the once beautiful land was now burnt through. Ahead of them, they saw nothing but burnt ground and smoke still rising in the distance.

"These lands used to be green and beautiful," Mondo said with a sad voice. The morning sky was a distinctive blue-red, as if the gods themselves were paying tribute to all the people that had died the night before.

As the children started looking around for clues, a white silhouette of a man suddenly appeared a few feet away from Tommy.

"Arrrrghhh!" shouted Tommy as he first caught sight of the man. With this, Mondo looked around and saw that it was his grandfather.

"Grandad!" he cried and ran over to him. "Where have you been? Why are you here?" Mondo's questions came quick and fast.

His grandfather then replied, "I have been waiting for you. I was here last night and saw you run off into the woods, so I waited".

This made Mondo even more confused.
"Wait. What? What do you mean? Where were you?" he asked.

His grandfather replied in his usually unclear way, "Well, I was here, there and everywhere."

"HOW?" Mondo then asked. After last night, his patience for Grandad's riddles was not as high as normal. His grandfather gave him a wink and then 'poof' he was gone. The three children were startled and started looking around everywhere.

Suddenly a voice said, "Over here!" and Mondo's grandfather was standing behind Tommy again.

Tommy looked around and screamed, "Arrggh!" for the second time. Mondo's grandfather started laughing.

"So, you can become invisible?" Mondo asked.

"Exactly," Grandad replied, seeming stranger than normal. "After your talk with me yesterday that name, Thornzan or Thorn rang a bell in my mind. So I decided to come and watch the whole thing in secret. I must say, I was very impressed with your magic last night children! Especially you Mondo; that ice dome was very impressive!"

The three children found themselves blushing at Grandad's words. He continued to tell the children about everything else he saw that night and how the people were powerless against the force of Thornzan's army.

"Why didn't you do something?" asked Jenny sadly.

"My fighting days are over," said Grandad.
"And besides, what good would I do against an entire army?"

Chapter 7
- Thornzan

"*A*nyway," continued Grandad, "I have waited around here because I needed to talk to you about their leader Thornzan. When I was young, I loved travelling through towns and getting to know the local people. Anyway, during one of my travels, I came to a town called Roseville and I met a young man called Thornzan. He had his own magic stand and he performed tricks for the local visitors and market folk. When he sensed that I was also a magician, he quickly sneaked over to me and wanted to introduce himself. He was interested in seeing if I wanted to join his secret magic club. They met every night in the cave above the town to practise magic. Anyway, I declined his offer because there was something about his eyes I did not like. Thornzan didn't give me another look and continued his show."

"That night, as I walked through the town, I could see the lights coming from the cave above the town. Thornzan must have been up there with his followers practising their magic. I remember thinking then, 'If he practises like that every night, he's going to be a very powerful wizard one day. If I'd known then that he was training an evil army up there, I would have put a stop to it. Anyway, the past is the past," Grandad said.

"Now!" he restarted, "If you want to go and find King Zoltar, I would start with that cave. Wizards don't like to change homes very often."

The group looked at each other, unsure whether or not they were ready for such a dangerous quest. Tommy still looked very jumpy.

Jenny was the first to speak, "I don't know if I want to go; I want to go home and be with my family."

With that, Mondo's grandfather told the children, "We don't know if anyone survived last night Jenny. After their 'little show here', they went to the village and burnt down all the houses."

With that the children wept, but they knew now that their path was clear. They had to go…

Chapter 8
– The Journey

*A*s the children prepared to go, Mondo's grandfather handed them a map to the cave. It looked like a long way away. He also said before they left, "Be wary on long journeys, for what you sometimes think you see might not always be so. Knowledge comes through thought and looking a little deeper."

As he stood there and waved goodbye to the children, Jenny said to Grandad, "Will you not come with us?"

"No, I must go to the capital and declare that war has begun and assemble the King's army. Besides, it's your time now." Mondo's grandfather replied.

He always seems so confident when he talks, Mondo thought.

As the group left town, they were surprised to see that everything outside the town was still lovely and green. The circus had not burnt everything they passed. Strange, Mondo thought.

After half a day's walk, the children approached the first town on the map Muddlegrass. From the outside the town seemed very nice: Big high walls and the sounds of working and children playing coming from inside. *Has the circus been here?* Mondo thought. As they neared the town however, they could see big stone doors, blocking any entrance into the town, and a sign saying 'Entrance 100zek'.

"100zek!" Tommy shouted out. "That's more than my Dad earns in a whole summer!"

After Tommy's loud shout came, "Hello?" and the children waited patiently. Round the corner walked two jester guards from Thornzan's army, all dressed in red and black.

"Do you have the 100zek for entrance?" one guard asked.

"No," the children replied.

"Well you better run along then," the guard replied. With that the children started running back from where they came.

The other guard quickly said, "Which town have you children come from?"

The children didn't answer and kept running until they reached the edge of the nearby woods.

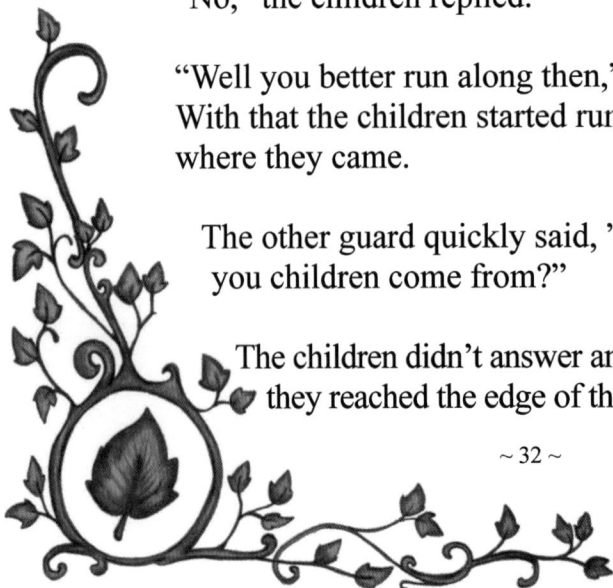

"You stupid fool!" the guard said. "You shouldn't have let them run off. Maybe they were the children Thorn is looking for!"

"Well, maybe they were just explorers?" the other guard replied.

"At that age!?!" the first guard said. "If we see them again, we must question them more." Both guards agreed.

The children, now hiding at the edge of the woods, had to come up with a plan, to find a way, to get past the guards.

"We should try to sneak around to the back of the wall and check out if there is another way to get into the town," suggested Jenny.

The children agreed and quickly ran round to the back side of the wall. However, as they approached the wall, they heard the guard jesters joking as they walked around the perimeter.

"OH NO!" said Mondo. "Here they come."

"What shall we do?" Tommy replied in panic.

The children were too far away from the nearby woods to run back so they were stuck!

Tommy nervously said to Mondo, "Do something!"

However, there was nothing Mondo could do, as making a big wall of ice suddenly appear would look too weird! Realising that there was no other choice, Jenny sighed and cast a magic spell on the three of them. This was something that she had never done before. The children were instantly

transformed. Jenny was transformed into a little tree, Mondo was transformed into a puddle of water and Tommy was transformed into… a chicken!!

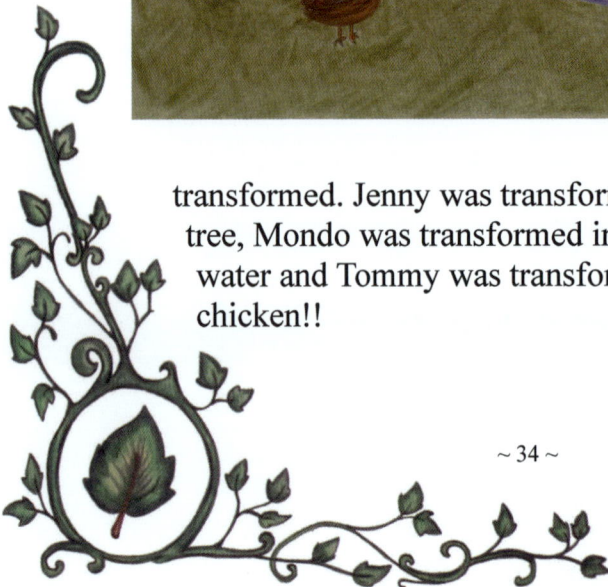

Jenny the tree looked at Tommy and laughed, "Hahaha! Suits your personality!" The little tree chuckled.

"Shhhh!" the Mondo the puddle said, "The guards are coming!"

As the guards came round the corner they seemed not to notice their new environment but they did notice one thing…

"A chicken!" one of the guards shouted!

"Let's get it!" the other replied.

So the two guards went chasing after Tommy as he clucked off into the wood. Jenny the tree shook with laughter and then transformed Mondo and herself back. They immediately started investigating the wall more. As Mondo touched the wall, it felt like a normal wall should: hard, gritty in texture and cold to touch. Mondo then thought back to what his grandfather had said about looking a little deeper and he cast ice into the stone. When the ice hit the stone, it gave off a green light.

Mondo touched the wall again, but this time he really pushed his hand into the stone. To his surprise, his hand started to go through the wall and it came out the other side. With one hand through, Mondo tried to push his face through next and then his whole body. Soon he was on the other side of the wall. Jenny then followed.

"It's a spell!" Jenny said.

As they looked around the town, there was nothing inside but burnt land and burnt buildings. No workers, no children, no people at all.

"It's a spell so no one knows what Thornzan is doing," said Mondo. "No wonder no one has ever said anything about the circus, no one was ever left alive to warn anyone! We must get going to the cave."

As Mondo and Jenny walked back through the wall, Tommy, still a chicken, was standing there waiting for them.

"Thanks!" he clucked sarcastically.

"I have never done any sort of spell like that before," said Jenny. "How was I to know you would be transformed into a chicken?"

"Where are the guards?" Mondo asked.

"I lost them," replied Tommy.

"Well we'd better get going before they come back," Mondo said.

On this the group agreed and they rushed off to the next town.

For the next few days, the children wandered from town to town on their way to the caves. Every town had the same high walls, the same noises coming from inside and the same 100zek sign with two guards. Every time the guards would go for their perimeter walk, Mondo would wait for them to be far enough away before he cast a ball of ice into the stone wall. If it shone green, he knew it was another fake town. All the towns on the way to Roseville were fake. This gave him a good feeling that they were on the right track.

Chapter 9
– The cave

*A*fter about a week of travelling, the group finally reached Roseville. It was late in the afternoon and the sky was a distinctive blue and red. The difference with this town was that it did not have a magical barrier around it like the others. This town, which laid below the cave, was burnt down and empty of life; that was clear to see. *Thornzan must have attacked this place first and then left it to symbolize his power,* Mondo thought.

"This town looks really evil," Tommy said with a trembling sound in his voice.

"Maybe that was the idea," Mondo replied.

"Have you never read any books?" Jenny said. "Villains' lairs are always the most evil place, everyone knows that!"

The three children climbed the hill and found what looked like an entrance to a cave. The strange thing here was that there were no jesters guarding the entrance of the cave, just a strange sound coming from inside. It was a high sound, then a low sound, repeating itself. The children entered the cave. As the children walked down the cave, it became cold and clammy and the repeating sound became louder and louder. As they continued through the cave, the light began to fade. Mondo was at the front, then Jenny, then Tommy. Soon they rounded a corner and came to a big opening where, in front of their eyes, slept the huge red dragon!

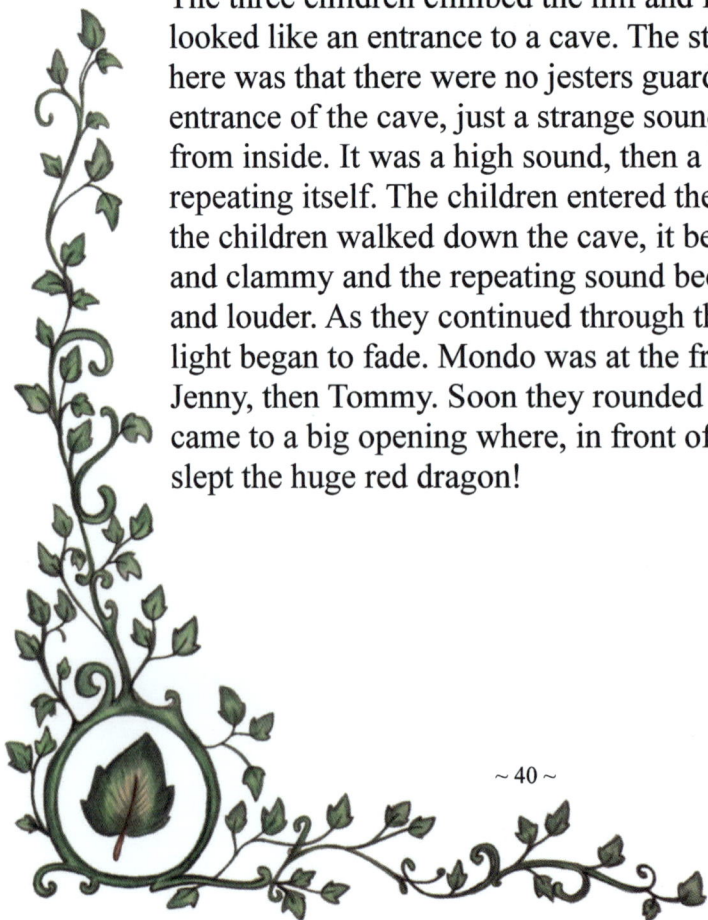

Behind the dragon, they could see King Zoltar locked up with six of his best knights, one from each town. At the sight of the huge, sleeping dragon, Tommy froze with fright and could not say anything; he just stood motionless.

Mondo whispered to Jenny, "Let's sneak over there and set the King free with your magic."

Jenny and Mondo began to sneak past the dragon and towards the King's cage while trying to keep as quiet as possible. While Jenny was sneaking, she was looking around for something to transform into a key to open the lock. As they approached the cage, she found a small stone on the floor and transformed it into a key so she could open the lock.

While Jenny was concentrating on unlocking the cage door with Mondo watching, Tommy was still standing lifelessly staring at the dragon. All of a sudden, Tommy saw the dragon open one eye. He then gave Tommy a sly smile and closed his eye again. Tommy tried to give out a scream to warn the others but nothing would happen; he was too scared!

He just kept repeating in his head *he's pretending, he's pretending, he's pretending, he's pretending. Must warn the others, must warn the others, must warn the others, must warn the others.* Tommy then closed his eyes, took a deep

breath and screamed, "HEEEEE'S

PRREEEEETEENDING!!!"

With the shout echoing around the walls, the dragon opened his eyes, stood up and charged at Mondo and Jenny.

Chapter 10
– The battle

As the dragon's big white teeth came flying at Mondo and Jenny, Mondo flung his arm over his head and turned away from the dragon. This created a dome of ice near the cage, which covered the two children. However the dragon's head came smashing into the dome of ice, shattering it to pieces. As the ice dome broke, Mondo and Jenny ran underneath the dragon's legs, away from the cage and back towards Tommy.

The dragon then breathed in and sent a ball of fire hurdling towards them! The dragon's fire was right behind the children, chasing them as they ran. Mondo grabbed Tommy and they ran around the corner. The ball of fire smashed into the wall and just missed them. The dragon moved towards them, breathed in and sent out a huge stream of fire at the children. This time, Mondo was ready! He stepped in front of Tommy and Jenny, put out his hands and sent a stream of ice towards the dragon. Mondo's ice and the dragon's fire hit each other like a massive explosion in the middle of the cave. The two elements seemed to be keeping each other at bay. They were as powerful as each other, but how would Mondo defeat the dragon?

As Mondo thought, he remembered something
his grandfather had told him about playing chess,
*"You hardly ever win a battle with your very
first move."* Mondo thought for a while, then
moved one of his hands out of the spell

and pointed it at the ground. As soon as he did this, his first spell weakened and the dragon's fire started coming closer and closer towards the three children and Mondo's hand. The heat of the fire started to become unbearable for the three of them. The dragon realised that he was close to victory so his attack became even more ferocious! As the fire came closer and closer to Mondo's hand he felt it start to burn, but the dragon didn't realize what was coming next.

From Mondo's other hand, which was pointed at the floor, a new stream of ice crept across the wet ground of the cave. It started to build up around the feet of the dragon. The dragon, still smelling near victory, didn't seem to notice as the ice slowly crept up his body. The children were barely being shielded by Mondo's ice and Mondo's hand was really hurting but he knew that as long as he did not stop pointing his other hand at the ground, victory would soon be theirs.

The ice continued to move up the dragon's body, but the dragon only seemed to realise when it reached his chest. In surprise and fear, the dragon tried to move but quickly found out he couldn't as the rest of his body was stuck in the ice.
The dragon ferociously tried to keep the fire coming at the children but Mondo's hands would not move.

The ice continued up the dragon's neck, into his mouth, down his throat and froze the fire inside the dragon's chest. The ice continued up the face until the whole dragon was frozen stiff. Mondo was victorious!

Realising the battle was over Mondo fell to the ground exhausted and put his burnt hand into a puddle. Tommy still stood still. It looked like he was taking it all in. Jenny ran over and released King Zoltar and his men. The King walked over to Mondo and picked him up. The group then walked together to the entrance of the cave. They stepped out to the edge of the hill overlooking the burnt town below.

King Zoltar thanked the children for their help.
However Mondo, Jenny and Tommy knew that this
was not the end, but just the beginning; as Thornzan
was still very much at large!

End of book 1

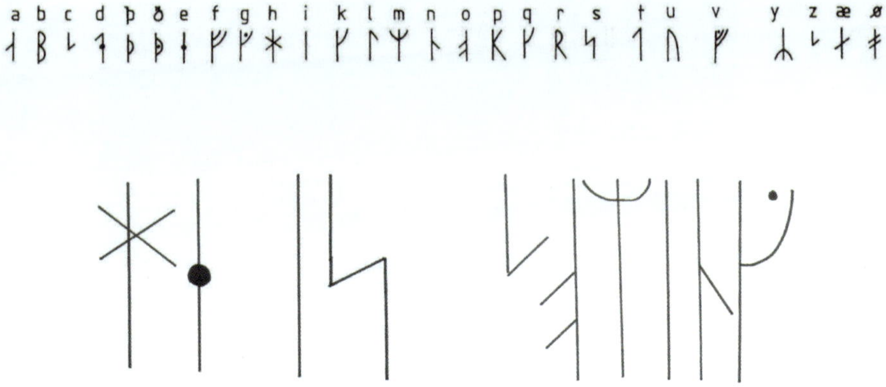
a b c d þ ð e f g h i k l m n o p q r s t u v y z æ ø

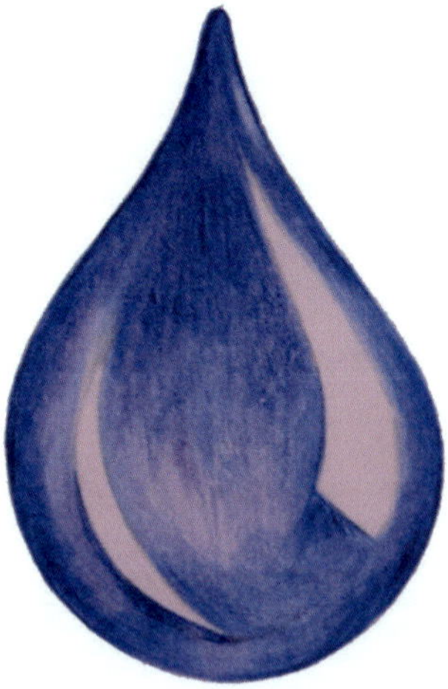

27304667R00028

Printed in Great Britain
by Amazon